SPECIAL OFFERS FOR MR MEN AND LITTLE MISS READERS

In every Mr Men and Little Miss book you will find a special token. Collect only six tokens and we will send you a super poster of your choice featuring all your favourite characters.

And for the first 4,000 readers we hear from, we will send you a Mr Men activity pad* and a bookmark* as well – absolutely free!

Return this page with six tokens from Mr Men and/or Little Miss books to:
Marketing Department, World International Publishing, Egmont House,
PO Box 111, 61 Great Ducie Street, Manchester M60 3BL.

Your name:_____

Address:_____

_____

_____ Postcode: _____

Signature of parent or guardian: _____

I enclose **six** tokens – please send me a Mr Men poster ☐

I enclose **six** tokens – please send me a Little Miss poster ☐

We may occasionally wish to advise you of other children's books that we publish. If you would rather we didn't, please tick this box ☐

*while stocks last   (Please note: this offer is limited to a maximum of two posters per household.)

Collect six of these tokens. You will find one inside every Mr Men and Little Miss book which has this special offer.

1 TOKEN

Please remove this page carefully

JOIN THE MR MEN & LITTLE MISS CLUB

Treat your child to membership of the long-awaited Mr Men & Little Miss Club and see their delight when they receive a personal letter from Mr Happy and Little Miss Giggles together with a great value Welcome Pack.

In the Pack they'll discover a unique collection of items for learning and fun: their own personal membership card; a club badge **with their name on**; an exclusive club members' cassette tape with two Mr Men stories and four songs; a copy of the excellent Fun To Learn™ Mr Men magazine; a great Mr Men sticker book; their own tiny flock model of Mr Happy; a club pencil; and, from the superb Mr Men range, a diary (with a padlock), an amazing bendy pen, an eraser, a book mark, and a key ring!

And that's not all. On their birthday and again at Christmas they'll get a card from the Mr Men and Little Misses. And every month the Mr Men magazine (available from newsagents) features exclusive offers for club members.

If all this could be bought in the shops you would expect to pay at least £12.00. But a year's membership is superb value at just **£7.99** (plus 70p postage). To enrol your child please send **your** name, address and telephone number together with **your child's** full name, date of birth and address (including postcode) and a cheque or postal order for £8.69 (payable to Mr Men & Little Miss Club) to: Mr Happy, Happyland (Dept. WI), PO Box 142, Horsham RH13 5FJ. Or call 01403 242727 to pay by credit card.

Please note: We reserve the right to change the terms of this offer (including the contents of the Welcome Pack) at any time but we offer a 14 day no-quibble money-back guarantee. We do not sell directly to children - all communications (except the Welcome Pack) will be via parents/guardians. After 31/12/96 please call to check that the price is still valid. Please allow 28 days for delivery. Promoter: Robell Media Promotions Limited, registered in England number 2852153.

little Miss Curious

by Roger Hargreaves

WORLD INTERNATIONAL
MANCHESTER

Little Miss Curious is a very curious
sort of person.

Just look at her house.

It's a very curious shape.

Isn't it?

Now look at her garden.

That's curious, too.

Isn't it?

Now look at Little Miss Curious.

She's rather curious looking, too.

And she also has a very curious
nature.

She wants to know the
how?
why?
and
what?
of everything.

One day, Little Miss Curious
set off for town.

"Why do doors squeak, but are not small
and furry with pink ears and long tails?"
she asked her door as she went out.

Understandably, the door didn't answer.

"Why do flowers live in beds but never sleep?" she asked the flowers in her garden.

They just smiled, knowingly.

Then she saw a worm.

"Why do worms in Nonsenseland wear bow-ties?" she asked.

"That's for me to know and you to find out about," said the worm, laughing.

Later, on the way to town,
Little Miss Curious met
Mr Nonsense.

Are you curious to find out
what she asked him?

Well go on then, turn over!

"I'm curious … " began Little Miss Curious,
" … to know why it is that sandwiches
are called sandwiches if they don't have
any sand in them."

"It just so happens," said Mr Nonsense,
"that this is a **sand** sandwich. I'm
rather partial to sand!"

"Happy Christmas," he said.

Then Mr Nonsense ran away holding his sandwich carefully so that the sand didn't fall out.

Little Miss Curious eventually arrived
in town.

Did I hear you ask, "Why?"

Well, you are curious,
aren't you?

But are you as curious as
Little Miss Curious?

Little Miss Curious had gone to
town to visit the library.

"I wonder, would you be able to
help me?" she asked

"Of course," said Mrs Page, the librarian.
"What are you looking for?"

"I'm looking for a book," began
Little Miss Curious,
"a book that will tell me
why the sky is blue ... "

" … and why combs have teeth,
but can't bite,
… and why chairs have legs,
but can't play football,
… and why … "

And she went on,
and on,
and on,
until there was a very long queue
behind her, that was growing longer
by the minute.

"That's enough!" cried Mrs Page.

"NEXT PLEASE!"

"But why … " Little Miss Curious started to ask.

But without quite knowing how or why,
she suddenly found herself out in the street.

"How curious," Little Miss Curious
thought to herself.

As she walked along the street,
Little Miss Curious asked herself:
"Why is everybody giving me
such curious looks?
And why is Little Miss Careful waving
her umbrella at me?
Is it because it's going to rain?"

We don't think so, do we?

Little Miss Curious ran off.

Are you going to ask, "Why?"

Are you becoming as curious as
Little Miss Curious?

Can you guess
where she ran off to?

Neither can I.

Come back Little Miss Curious
and tell us where you're going!

You see, we're all ever so curious.

Yes, really we are!